ASHES TO ASHES

DEATH IN THE AGE OF TRUMP

PAUL BOUCHARD

Paul Bouchard is the author of more than a dozen books
to include the novels Enlistment and Priya's Choice.

ASHES TO ASHES
DEATH IN THE AGE OF TRUMP

This is a work of fiction. All of the characters, names, incidents,
organizations, and dialogue in this novel are either the products
of the author's imagination or are used fictitiously.

iUniverse books may be ordered through booksellers or by contacting:

iUniverse
1663 Liberty Drive
Bloomington, IN 47403
www.iuniverse.com
844-349-9409

ISBN: 978-1-6632-2931-1 (sc)
ISBN: 978-1-6632-2932-8 (e)

Library of Congress Control Number: 2022900505

Print information available on the last page.

iUniverse rev. date: 02/11/2022

For our wounded warriors

I knew it wouldn't end well, but I never thought this: my best friend, Eric, dead, his ashes in an urn some three feet from me. The urn is in his girlfriend's Cecilia's book bag.

Cecilia and I are in my old 2008 Subaru Forester heading north on I-95, I behind the wheel, she in the front passenger seat, her blue book bag on the floor board between her legs, the urn in her bag. Destination: Bangor, Maine, Eric's hometown. His funeral will be this Sunday.

It's Friday, January 8, 2021, and we're just outside the beltway. A half hour ago, I informed Cecilia that it would be better if we headed north on I-270, then I-70, through Pennsylvania, to avoid the heavy New York City traffic, but she said she really wanted to "see the New York City skyline," so I relented, no pushback.

The last forty-eight hours have been absolutely crazy. Eric had called me from Bangor this past Sunday. "I'll be in town this week. Big Trump rally on Wednesday, bud. I don't want to miss it."

"Cool. Do you need a ride down?"

"Nope. Figured you'd ask, but I'm good. Dad hooked me up. Knows a local long-haul truck driver heading south to Florida. The truck driver, his name is Bill Palmer, told me he'll drop me off on I-395 outside DC."

"Nice. Works for me. Where exactly off I-395, so I can pick you up?"

"Spoiler alert, dude. No need for you to pick me up."

"You're kidding. No way."

"Way. Found me some chick on the internet. Hard-core Trumpette. We hit it off the last ten days. Plenty of photos and video coverage. I give her a solid seven out of ten on the rating scale. Her name's Cecilia. She said she'll pick me up by Uber. I got it all figured out, buddy."

The Trump rally was two days ago. Eric insisted I meet him there on Capitol grounds, he and Cecilia constantly texting me to give me their location amongst the enormous crowd. I finally found them some three hundred feet from the stage where President Trump was addressing his supporters—hard-core zealots, if you ask me. Eric was all smiles. Dressed in a sweater and a thick jean jacket, he had a large American flag rigged to his wheelchair, with a tall pennant declaring Combat Disabled Veteran next to the flag. Cecilia was in blue jeans, a gray sweatshirt, and a heavy black leather jacket, and she had an American flag bandana prominently covering her forehead. The three of us were wearing face masks on account of Covid-19, but most of the protesters were maskless.

Eric's wheelchair was the result of his combat injury in Afghanistan last year. An IED hit his convoy, and he lost both his legs, making him a double amputee.

I first met Eric in 2018 when we did basic training together at Fort Leonard Wood, Missouri. I never met a more talented person than Eric, and he quickly became my best friend.

How did he die? Simple: when Trump finished his disjointed all-over-the place whining session, he told his die-hard supports to "take back your capitol," or words to that effect. Eric and Cecilia were all pumped up and started following the crowd forward. Me, I told the new love birds, "Gang, I'm heading out. I'm not interested in this, and I don't have a good feeling about it."

"Ah, don't be a pussy, Dean," Eric told me.

"Eric, it's great seeing you, man. And nice to meet you, Cecilia, but I'm outta here."

"Everything President Trump said is true," Cecilia insisted, and she started pushing Eric's wheelchair forward. "This election was stolen from Trump, from us. Our president won by a landslide."

"Well, maybe or maybe not, but I'm outta here. Eric, call or text me anytime."

"OK, buddy, but you are a pussy. C'mon man, this is great. This is our moment." He then realized that I was serious and not backing down. "OK. And yeah, I'll be calling you, probably Friday. I'm staying over Cecilia's apartment for the remainder of the week, but I'll need a ride back to Bangor this weekend."

"Sure. Too easy." I ended with, "Be careful out there. There's some nut cases here. I've seen quite a few protesters wearing military fatigues and protective equipment. My guess is they're not only trained in combatives, but they're carrying weapons, packing heat."

I remember Cecilia responding with, "The president told us to go to the Capitol, so we're doing what we're told."

Eric was all smiles. He said, "Kiss me, babe," and Cecilia bent down and kissed him on the lips. The last words Eric spoke to me were "Later, dude."

Eric was part of the protestors who made it inside the Capitol. The way Cecilia explained it, she and Eric had no trouble moving forward, not with his prominent flag and disabled combat veteran pennant. Cecilia would later tell me, "A couple of big guys picked up his wheelchair, with Eric in it, and they brought him all the way into the Capitol. I followed."

I learned that once things got crazy inside, shots were fired, and as bad luck would have it, a stray bullet hit Eric in the chest. It was a fatal shot.

Cecilia insists a Capitol Guard police officer killed Eric "deliberately and without provocation," is how she worded it, but I haven't read the police report—things are still being investigated, but boy did things move fast.

Less than two hours after Eric's fatal wound, I got a call from Cecilia. She was surprisingly calm and very straightforward. "Eric's dead," she told me.

"Cecilia, don't play games, man. What's going on? I picked up the news on my iPhone that the Capitol building was breached. What's going on?"

"I'm telling you, Dean, Eric's dead. I'm at George Washington University Hospital. The Capitol Police killed Eric."

I was stunned and speechless.

"I've ID'd the body. Next is an autopsy. There's a forensic photographer taking tons of photos too. Eric was declared dead fifteen minutes ago. Cops are investigating the matter, and they're also calling next of kin as we speak."

I was silent.

"Meet me at the morgue," and she gave me the morgue address. I was there in forty-five minutes.

It was when I was at the morgue that I received a call from Eric's father, David. David Holzer, together with his wife, Lynn, Eric's mom, are the top-selling real estate agents in Bangor and its surrounding towns. Eric's dad has always been calm and smooth and logical and articulate, skills that no doubt led to his financial success.

"Dean, you take care of my son, you hear?"

"Yessir."

"You were his best friend, and we consider you part of the family." He paused. "We want Eric cremated."

"OK."

"I've already made arrangements for his funeral. It will be this Sunday, inside the Bangor High School Auditorium, at two p.m. Coach Frank Scagliotta told me they'll be retiring Eric's number, something they've apparently been planning for some time."

"Yessir."

"Now Lynn and I have already researched this, and the best place for cremation around DC is …"

And on it went like that, Mr. Holzer in his logical, planned, matter-of-fact way, and me memorizing his detailed plan, which included my assurances that Eric's brain, after the autopsy—which Mr. Holzer also arranged for—would be donated to "Dr. Daniel Pearl. He's a neuropathologist who will assist with the autopsy. I saw

5

Dr. Pearl on *60 Minutes* once. I just got off the phone with him. The autopsy will be at …"

Eric was cremated yesterday, and here we are, me and Cecilia, heading north, Eric's ashes in an urn in a book bag.

'll never forget the first time I met Eric. Our basic training company had just finished our first timed two-mile run. Eric and I were in first platoon, I in the second squad, he in the fourth. I had seen him before, but we had never met. After that first timed run, Eric finished first by a wide margin, and I snuck in third. A slim muscular Black guy everybody called Rock came in second. Eric, all six feet and two hundred pounds of him, ran the two miles in twelve minutes and thirty seconds. Rock came in twenty seconds later, and I was just shy of thirteen minutes. Later that day, both Eric and I got assigned to KP, kitchen police, wiping down mess hall tables and mopping mess hall floors. During one of our many breaks, we struck up a conversation.

"Nice run out there this morning," I told him.

"Thanks. Yeah, it went well. I can do better though. I'll go faster next time."

"Dude, I saw the height and weight charts. How can a guy like you who weighs two hundred pounds run that fast for that long?"

"I just do it, that's all."

"Me and Rock, we both weigh around a buck fifty, and you crushed us."

That's when Eric informed me he had recently been a college football star at the University of Maine. He graduated in 2016 and was invited to the invitational combine. The Cleveland Browns and New England Patriots were the most interested teams, but there were others too. And he had firm offers from many of the Canadian Football League teams.

"The Montreal Alouettes offered me a contract," he told me as we were filling up salt shakers, "but my dream was always to play in the NFL, so I turned them down and waited on the NFL."

I learned that the Cleveland Browns signed him up on the practice squad. "I was doing really well, the coaches telling me the front office was writing a contract. But then I injured my shoulder. My legs were fine, but my left shoulder got heavily bruised. I'm coming back though, Specialist Leonard. My dad called me last week saying the Seahawks are giving five players a tryout, and I'm one of the five."

"Wow, that's awesome, Specialist Holzer. Man, with all of that, why did you join the army?"

"I get that question pretty often," he told me, "but I'm sure you've heard the same. Word in the platoon is Specialist Leonard is a lawyer."

"That's true, I am a lawyer. I practice media law for Bloomberg News out of Baltimore. I simply wanted to join the JAG Corps as a reservist to do my part of public service. The JAG recruiter told me my packet was declined because the other applicants 'all had army experience.' He recommended I enlist in the army, serve two or three years in my local National Guard or Reserve unit, then reapply to the JAG Corps. So that's why I'm here. I didn't sign up for active duty. I'm one of the Reserve recruits."

"You don't say?" Eric told me. "Same here. I signed up with my local National Guard unit."

"Why?"

"Dude, I want to do something for my country, like you, public service. Our nation is at war right now, and I want to do my part. All the famous baseball players and football players and other athletes of the day, when the nation was at war, they answered the call. Ted Williams, Joe DiMaggio, the great Jackie Robinson who broke the color barrier. When World War Two broke out, they served. The football greats did the same. You know who my real hero is, right?"

"No. Educate me."

"Pat Tillman, dude. Great football player. Signed for millions. Decided to take a time out to serve his country. He gave his life, you know."

"Yeah, I know."

"He's my hero. And my role model."

I remember there was a pause in our conversation, then Eric said, "I know I have a real shot at the NFL. And I've received firm offers from the Canadian Football League again. Like you, I'll be a weekend warrior. I can play in the NFL while doing a National Guard weekend drill here and there. Look at the great David Robinson, the all-star NBA basketball player who was a naval academy grad. When San Antonio drafted him, he simply shifted to the Reserves and did his obligatory military service in the off-season. I'll be doing the same."

"Sounds like a plan."

"Yeah. By the way, what's your first name?"

"Dean," I told him.

"Dean, I'm Eric. Pleased to meet you. Anyway, that's the game plan, the NFL. My left shoulder is stronger than ever. That's why Seattle called. I joined my local guard unit so I could serve. The opening my unit had was in public affairs. Our unit's slated to deploy to Afghanistan in six months. I graduate here, do the AIT advanced individual training, get signed by the Seahawks, then I'll deploy. I've got it all figured out, and when I get back from my deployment, I'll be playing for Seattle."

"Your guard unit is a public affairs detachment?"

"Yes, that's right. English and history were always my favorite subjects in high school and college. I don't mean to toot my own horn, but I've got plans to write a novel too. I was the editor of my high school newspaper, and I was a staff writer for the UMaine paper. Writing's my thing. Heck, after my NFL career, I might follow in your footsteps, Dean, and go to law school. I'd love to be a sports agent."

"What was your major?" I asked him.

"Dah. C'mon Dean, grow a brain," he said jokingly. "Journalism, dude. I've got it all planned out."

"You sure do. So you'll be joining a PAO, a public affairs office or detachment."

"Right."

"And your unit's deploying?"

"Yeah, that's right. I've been told that when you deploy, you do a lot of things like vehicle maintenance, pull security, whatever. But we'll also be running an online newsletter and writing press releases. And speeches, too, for the higher-ups."

"I see. So what's your MOS?" I asked him.

"Dude, reporter. Forty-six Quebec."

"You don't say?" I said. "Same as mine. Cool."

"Wow. Really cool. Say, so your AIT after basic is the Defense Information School?" He was now wiping down a table.

"Yep. Right in my neck of the woods. DINFOS it is, at Fort Meade, Maryland. I live in Laurel, just outside the base and not too far from Baltimore."

So that's how we met. Luck, serendipity, whatever, we had a lot in common. Word got around the platoon and the company that one Specialist Eric Holzer had successfully tried out for the NFL but got injured, had been a college football star as a running back, and had firm offers from the CFL and a tryout with the Seahawks after he completed basic and AIT. No one had better PT scores—physical training scores —than Eric. A 12:15 two-mile time, 110 pushups and 105 sit-ups, the latter two events timed in two-minute increments. Holzer was a beast, and the scholar-athlete type, often talking about books, and politics, and history, especially sports history. Soon, his nickname became Top Dawg. Also The Stud, but mostly Top Dawg. Me, everybody was calling the Fast Lawyer, because I could run two miles in around thirteen minutes. And I was getting a lot of lawyer questions from fellow basic trainees, and also from the drill sergeants, mostly about family law matters because some of the guys were going through divorces or paternity and child custody disputes. Fast Lawyer, Free Consultations—that was the word.

"Dean, can we stop at the next highway rest stop?" Cecilia asks.

"Sure," I tell her. "I think the next one is in fifteen miles or so. We recently passed the sign for it."

"Thanks."

Cecilia's been quiet, her white earbuds plugged into her iPhone, listening to who knows what—music, probably. She had taken out one of the earbuds to ask for the rest stop. I could use a comfort break too. And a Starbucks refill. In ten minutes we reach the rest stop. Then we're back on I-95, in northern Maryland, close to the Delaware border. When we cross the state line and pass the Welcome to Delaware sign, Cecilia, removing her earbuds, says, "Delaware sucks. Home of President Biden. We all know he stole the election. As far as I'm concerned, Biden can bite me. Plus, he's corrupt. Ever hear of Peter Schweizer?"

"Actually, I have," I tell her truthfully. "I saw him on *60 Minutes* once."

"Good. Schweizer's all over it. None of the fake news bullshit."

I say nothing. My mind returns to my deceased best friend, and Cecilia returns to her plugged-ear listening pleasure.

I t was no surprise that Eric would win all the awards at basic training. Physical Fitness Award, Leadership Award, Top Soldier. Top Dawg won them all, and rightfully so.

I remember maybe halfway through basic when Eric and I were cleaning our M16s after a firing range practice and Drill Sergeant Smith approached us.

You couldn't miss Drill Sergeant Smith, all six feet six of him. Tall, bald, always wearing sunglasses, always chewing tobacco, a spittoon in his hand, and his Popeye forearms both tattooed with colored American flags.

"Well, well, if it isn't the two pencil-pushing dicks. What a shame. Soldiers with two of the fastest run times in the company, but they won't go infantry. A waste to Uncle Sam's army. How you pukes doing? And clean those precious weapons real good now."

"Fine, Drill Sergeant," we told him.

"Y'all know I'm just giving you boys the shit. Leonard the Lawyer, that's cool. Everybody needs a lawyer at some point. And Holzer, you Top Dawg. Good luck with that NFL tryout, stud." I remember him spitting some chewed tobacco not in his spittoon but on the ground, since we were out in the field near the firing range. Drill Sergeant Smith then told us, "Me, I went as far as I could with football. Played at West Virginia, a great team. Second string tight end. Played two years, but then I hurt my back. Didn't care much for college without football, so I took a year off. My back healed, but not quite enough for the pounding on the football field. But good enough for Uncle Sam's army."

"West Virginia University has great football," Eric said as we continued cleaning our weapons.

"Oh yeah. And I've got to tell you, stud," Drill Sergeant Smith continued as he looked at Eric, "I can't understand how some two-hundred pounder like you can run two miles in a bit over twelve minutes."

"Well I guess I'm like Billy Beane, Drill Sergeant."

"Who?"

"Billy Beane. The great general manager and former big leaguer Michael Lewis wrote about in the bestseller *Moneyball*. Made a movie about it too. Brad Pitt played Billy Beane."

"Never heard of that book," Smith said. "And I haven't seen the movie. I don't read much actually. Bit of Stephen King here and there. I figure you pencil dicks read a fair amount, given y'all gonna be army writers. Shame you pukes ain't going infantry."

"Well, Drill Sergeant," Eric said, "maybe there's truth to the saying that the pen is mightier than the sword."

Smith, with a big wad of chewing tobacco in his stretched left cheek, said, "Man, whatever dipshit came up with that nonsense is big-time wrong. Give me a sword and give me a pen, and I'll take the sword and chop up the fucking pen every time. Sword wins, pukes. Pen loses."

Eric shifted gears. "Speaking of Stephen King, Drill Sergeant, you know I'm also from his hometown, Bangor, Maine."

"That's cool."

"Yeah. I've seen him a few times, too. Tall guy. I can't say I'm a big fan of his genre, horror, but I recognize and admire his talent. And he's so prolific."

"Good stuff. I like some of his books. The movies too."

"So who's your favorite writer, Drill Sergeant?" Eric asked.

"Can't say that I have one. Maybe Stephen King. Tom Clancy too. How about you, pukes?"

"My favorite is Philip Roth," Eric said.

"Never heard of him," Smith said, again spitting some tobacco on the ground. "The only Roth I know is Roth IRA. Got one of those for me and one for my wife. Wife number two, actually. Wife number one didn't work out. I got it right the second time, though. Got me a mail-order bride straight from the Philippines. Gorgeous tight little ass on my sweetheart, lemme tell ya. She makes some awesome pork adobo, too. Yep, four more years, pukes, then I'm retiring with my gorgeous Filipina to the outskirts of Spokane, Washington. Plenty of good hunting and fishing there, and my hot babe Filipina will make me plenty of that pork adobo. And deer and elk adobo too."

Good memories, man. One never forgets a guy like Drill Sergeant Smith. And everyone, including all the drill sergeants, was impressed with Eric. There was plenty to be impressed with—Eric shot expert with the M16, threw the grenades perfectly, did all the tasks and tested skills to perfection, and, as predicted, won all the awards at basic training. What a training cycle he had. And toward the end of basic, Eric informed me that not only the Seahawks but also the Texans were giving him a tryout.

"The NFL running back average for forty yards is 4.49," he once told me, meaning seconds for the timed forty-yard event. "I'm consistently coming in at 4.47, 4.48. I guess when you've got run times like mine, the NFL will come calling."

Eric wasn't a braggart, but he wasn't low-key about his accomplishments either. The subject reminds me of a saying about the great Cardinals pitcher, Dizzy Dean, who once purportedly said, "If it's the truth, it's not bragging." The truth was, Eric was the Top Dawg.

After he graduated from basic with all those awards, the next stop was AIT at Fort Meade, Maryland. Eric and I flew together from Saint Louis to Baltimore-Washington International, where a van brought us to Fort Meade and DINFOS, the Defense Information School.

Neither our parents nor our girlfriends came to our graduation at basic. I told my parents it made no sense to travel to the middle of Missouri when my next army training school was right at home between DC and Baltimore. Plus Stephanie, also an attorney, had a big deposition to prep for. "I'll be home shortly anyway, babe," I told her.

Eric's situation was similar. His real estate power-couple parents had a big sale going on during graduation weekend, and his then girlfriend, Lori, a biology student at UMaine, had exams around the corner that needed plenty of study time.

DINFOS was a lot different from basic. Our DINFOS class had all of the military branches represented—army, navy, air force, marines, also coast guard—and we army soldiers did our physical training (PT) in the morning before our journalism classes; the marines did PT thrice a week, while the other branches seemed to never do it. Eric and I were roommates at DINFOS and—

***

"Dean, can we stop for another comfort break?" Cecilia asks me, one of her earbuds out.

"Sure. Good timing. And I actually like New Jersey. The best state to drive through. Plenty of rest stops, and a gas station attendant pumps your gas."

Our comfort break lasted some thirty minutes. Cecilia bought chips and a soda, and I filled up with a sausage sandwich and coffee, both from Dunkin' Donuts.

After tipping the service station attendant, I'm back on the highway heading north, Cecilia munching on her chips and listening to her tunes.

D INFOS was a busy ten-week academic setting with plenty of graded assignments in public affairs, photography, and journalism, the latter accounting for a full 70 percent of a student's final grade. After two weeks in the program, all army students with at least a 75 average were given weekend passes.

Given Fort Meade's proximity to northern Virginia, where my parents live in Annadale, I invited Eric over to my parents' home a couple of times, and they liked him from the start. Eric also met my then girlfriend, Stephanie, a labor lawyer based in Richmond, a few times, also at my parents' home.

My relationship with Stef had never reached solid traction, even before I shipped out for basic training. An incredibly beautiful, smart, ambitious sort, Stef was working crazy hours at a prestigious Richmond law firm, determined to make partner. With that, we rarely saw each other. Plus, geography was really a problem, as I lived in Laurel, Maryland, a traffic-heavy three-hour drive from Richmond. The end to our relationship was brought about by a headhunter agency, without Stef's knowledge or application, contacting her out of the blue with an offer from a Silicon Valley firm offering big bucks, relocation costs, and a partner-track position. It was an offer she couldn't refuse, so she took it. This was midway during DINFOS.

'll never forget our fifth weekend off at DINFOS, the weekend Eric and I decided to fly up to Bangor and visit his folks and sister, Wendy, then a senior in high school entertaining acceptances from Bowdoin, Colby, and Cornell. Though the first two colleges would have left her in her native state, she would go with her first choice, Ivy League Cornell.

It was my first time in Maine, and I loved the scenery, especially the lack of traffic. Eric's parents and sister were great and welcoming, we ate steak and lobster twice, and I got introduced to two fine restaurants, McLaughlin's Seafood and The Fiddlehead Restaurant. I know I'll have plenty of time off tomorrow, and I plan on patronizing those two eateries.

As for DINFOS, it was challenging, and the grading was strict, but Eric and I both managed to sneak onto the Commandant's List, reserved for the top 20 percent of the class.

Besides the visits to our parents' homes, Eric and I crashed a few of the popular DINFOS weekend hotel parties, where a bunch of students would get a hotel room, drink beer, eat pizza, and hook up. So many of the girls were interested in the scholar-athlete-future NFLer, but Eric remained loyal to Lori, and I wasn't quite ready to play the field.

That was all in late 2018 and early 2019. Toward the end of that year I met Barbara, a mortgage broker in Annapolis. I met her shortly after graduation from

DINFOS, through a colleague at work who was dating her sister. A true sweetheart, Barbara would be here with me right now if it wasn't for the fact that she hasn't received the Covid-19 vaccine yet. "You know I don't go where there are crowds, honey," she keeps telling me. "Including funerals." This also explains why Barbara didn't attend the Trump rally two days ago (besides the fact that Barbara despises Trump). Luckily, I got the one-shot Johnson & Johnson Covid-19 vaccine two weeks ago through my employer's insurance. I still wear a mask, but not when in this car. Cecilia's informed me, "I've been tested a few times, and I always come up negative. I don't believe in vaccines. It's all a hoax. Look at Sweden. They're doing better than us and they didn't shut down the country. Sometimes even a socialist country gets it right."

S lightly to the right, many miles away, I can see the New York City skyline, and I notice Cecilia sees it too. Traffic is relatively light, and we're making good time. New York City roughly marks the halfway point to Bangor. With that, I figure our ETA—estimated time of arrival—is around 10 p.m.

When we graduated from DINFOS, Eric's plan came to fruition just as predicted—he tried out with two NFL teams, the Seahawks and the Texans. While I was back at work for Bloomberg News—a great company that was kind enough to grant me unpaid leave so I could complete basic and DINFOS—I kept receiving constant texts from Eric about his tryout performances.

"All great here. Passed the physical. Great run times. Ran a 4.46 forty. Couldn't have a better tryout."

That's how I remember the Seattle one, and Houston was no different. In the end, Seattle gave him a slot on their practice squad for 2020, but Houston upped that with a firm one-year contract for a lot of money. If memory serves, it was for half a million dollars. This was in early March of 2020, and Houston wanted him to report to camp in September of that year, right after his six-month deployment. Some unit deployments are for a full year, some even extend a few months to make it a fourteen-month deployment, and some deployments are six months or less, depending on one's unit. Eric's unit was slated to deploy to Afghanistan from late March to late September 2020.

Deploy he did. I remember Eric sending texts and photos by cellphone of his unit's flight from Bangor

International Airport heading first to Ireland, then to some undisclosed locations, with the final destination being Afghanistan. Eric was certainly cognizant of the military rules about social media postings and military locations (basically, never post your location, and never post any sensitive information that could give our enemies any advantages). Eric was kosher with all of that, which explains why I would receive plain emails from him like, "facilities good, adequate accommodations … I'm eating well … I'm staying in shape … I'm living the dream— deploy, then NFL, baby … wrote a press release today …"

He would never divulge the subject matter of that press release.

The news of some virus called corona from China was always in the news, but POTUS Trump and others told us not to worry. Little did they know just how much of a game changer it would be. By mid-March, my employer mandated that the bulk of us employees work from home on account of the virus. Same thing happened with Barbara's mortgage brokerage—a directive to work from home.

Eric's emails from downrange were steady, energetic, and optimistic. "I want to be where the action is," he wrote in an email. "By the way, no worries here about Covid-19. We all wear masks."

Eric informed me he went on convoys where he and other soldiers delivered needed supplies like protective masks and hand sanitizer to the Afghan army and villages. He wrote stories about these goodwill trips, and he told me there wasn't much to do, so every time he got a chance to "go outside the wire," he did. His emails always ended with, "Living the Dream, Eric."

But then, on a routine convoy, one Eric had done half a dozen times, the Humvee he was in got hit by an IED. He and some other injured soldiers were medevacked as soon as possible, got the best care that could be provided at a MASH unit, and subsequently were flown to an American military hospital in Germany, where both his legs—the legs that had supported his two-hundred pound frame, the legs that propelled his incredible speed and power, the legs that plowed through defenders, gained yardage, and crossed so many times into the end zone, the legs that made him a local football legend and earned him a college scholarship and then a half-a-million dollar NFL contract—those legs had to be amputated. Gone now, ending all the professional football dreams they had so faithfully supported and carried for many years.

I suspected something had gone wrong when I hadn't received an email from Eric in more than a week. My worst fears were realized when I received the saddest of calls from the normally stoic David Holzer, Eric's dad, the self-made millionaire real estate broker and investor, who choked up intermittently as he informed me of Eric's tragic injury.

Stunned, speechless, mad, sad—a whole range of emotions overcame me. When the phone call ended, I drank half a bottle of wine, three beers, and two glasses of cognac. Luckily it was a Friday night, so I didn't have to work the next day. I remember sitting in my recliner, drinking away, my flat-screen on ESPN SportsCenter and muted, and there, scrolling at the bottom of the screen, was the incredible coincidental notice of "Eric Holzer, 24, Texans signee injured in combat in Afghanistan."

During that saddest and hardest of phone calls, Eric's dad had given me the phone number to Eric's room at the military hospital in Germany. I called Eric on a Saturday, the day after I spoke with the senior Holzer. Eric was surprisingly calm. He explained what happened matter-of-factly, said one of the four soldiers on the Humvee, a Sergeant Robinson from Wisconsin, didn't make it, that he, Eric, was experiencing some mild ringing in his ears, and that he was diagnosed with a traumatic brain injury, but "my meds for the TBI help me out a lot." I remember him saying, "Hey, buddy, I'll be in your neck of the woods soon. Walter Reed Medical Center. Right in DC."

"I'll be sure to visit, Eric. Often."

"Thanks, Bud. Mom and Dad and Wendy and Lori will be visiting too. I'm glad to be alive, Dean, lemme tell you."

Not once did we speak about his amputations or football.

Nearly a month after the injury itself, Eric was at Walter Reed, a forty- to-sixty-minute drive from my apartment in Laurel, depending on traffic. And like I had told him over the phone on more than one occasion, I saw him regularly, two to three times a week, actually.

Eric's physical therapy went well and lasted nearly a month. His tinnitus was subsiding, and the meds for his TBI seemed to be working. As the days turned to weeks, he showed a lot of improvement with his prosthetic legs, but I noticed he preferred just getting around in his wheelchair, something he was good at, since he hadn't lost much of his upper body strength. Instead of those former powerful legs of his, now his broad shoulders and strong arms and hands would get him around. My visits to Eric were pleasant and usually one hour in duration. Never did we broach the subject of football.

Eric's last Saturday at Walter Reed culminated with his birthday, his twenty-fifth. Barbara, Eric's family, and I (all of us wearing protective masks on account of the Covid-19 virus) were in attendance, along with a special guest, retired army Colonel Gregory Gadson, the one-time West Point football star and himself a similar double-leg amputee. We all ate birthday cake, talked about Eric's upcoming home in Bangor, and listened to Colonel Gadson's heartfelt words of encouragement, the most important one being, "Always find a purpose in your life. There's always something to do and to live for."

Days later, Eric's family transported him home to Bangor, and just before he left, I insisted I'd be there that weekend for the big event.

The big event was on a Saturday in late August. Barbara and I drove up to Bangor and witnessed the incredible support of Eric's family, community, National Guard unit, his alma mater the University of Maine, the Wounded Warriors Project, and Habitat for Humanity. The event was a big welcome home to Eric in the form of a brand-new three-bedroom house along the Penobscot River, minutes from his parents' home. (Barbara and I wore masks at all times and kept sanitizing our hands; if Barbara had known about the huge turnout, I doubt she would have attended).

Eric's parents—the real estate professionals that they are—purchased the once vacant lot and oversaw the construction of the Cape Cod-style home with a nice wraparound porch, a house that took just one month to complete, all accomplished during Eric's recuperation at Walter Reed. The Wounded Warrior nonprofit funded the project, D'Angelo Builders as the general contractor provided construction labor along with plenty of volunteers from the local Habitat for Humanity chapter, and both Home Depot and Lowes chipped in with free or heavily discounted building materials. Both Bangor's young mayor, Clare Davitt, and Maine's governor, the energetic Janet Mills, in her early seventies, attending the welcome-home ceremony. Both politicians spoke well and briefly, as did Eric's National Guard commander, Colonel Roy.

Eric, his girlfriend Lori, Eric's parents, and Wendy, all held the giant scissors that clipped the wide blue ribbon welcoming Eric and Lori into their new home. (Eric and Lori weren't married, but according to Eric's mom, "marital discussions" were "in the air.") The festivities on that warm, sunny August day ended with yet another surprise, this one in the form of a brand-new Chevy Equinox courtesy of the Wounded Warriors Project, fully equipped with accelerator and brake pedals on the steering wheel instead of on the floorboard. Eric, Lori, Barbara, and I went for a spin around town, with Eric behind the wheel, driving well in his new wheels. Eric's dad later told me, "Eric's good to drive short distances, but because of his medications, he can't drive long trips. Thirty-minutes back and forth, tops."

All was well with Eric in early-to-mid August, but then things took a downturn. His TBI was getting worse, and his meds had to be changed, dosage and type. The doctors said, "New combinations have to be tried out." Eric was now forgetful, his conversations weren't fluid, and as a result, he was getting easily frustrated and agitated.

I went to see him one weekend in early September and noticed Lori would make him write things down on Post-it notes so he would remember stuff like, "get screwdriver in garage to tighten an outlet screw."

Some of the guys from Eric's National Guard unit had just gotten back from their Afghan tours, and that Saturday we met at Eric's new home for a game of poker and to watch UFC fights on Fox Sports1. I didn't think alcohol was a good idea because of Eric's meds, but some of the guys bought Jack Daniels and beer, so it was hard not to partake, even for Eric. Early into the poker game, I noticed Eric was off, thinking he had a straight when he didn't and saying "two pairs beats a set—I win" when it's an inferior hand. He was drinking beer when he probably shouldn't have been, and his agitation grew as the night progressed. We decided to end the game and focus on the UFC fights, and that was better. I remember we guests left quietly late that night. I returned to my hotel room and drove back to Laurel the next day. All along the eleven-hour trip that Sunday, I kept thinking about Eric's decline.

Eric's condition unfortunately continued to decline. Lori knew she could always text or call me, and likewise I could text and call her.

One Thursday night she texted me with, "Eric's more and more frustrated, and aggressive. He throws things around sometime. Fortunately, not at me, but I'm getting scared."

With that, I decided to drive up to Bangor to pay Eric a visit and check things out. My visit was a repeat of my earlier one: I stayed at the same hotel, Courtyard by Marriott, and Eric's National Guard battle buddies and I went to Eric's house for more poker, pizza, wings, beer and whiskey, and sports on TV. I noticed Eric was more forgetful—he always had a pen and a small yellow pad of Post-its next to him now—but there was no aggression.

That all changed the next day, a Sunday, when I was driving back to Maryland. Lori called me, and I had my cellphone hands-free on speaker.

"Hi, Dean."

"Hey, Lori. What's up?"

"I know you're driving south. Are you close to your apartment?"

"Well, I'm in Pennsylvania. I got another three hours or so of driving. Why? What's going on?"

"Well, just to let you know, Eric got aggressive again."

"Oh no. What happened?"

"Not on me, thank God. It's our great Buck."

"Buck? The beautiful German shepherd? Eric loves that dog."

"Yeah. Buck stays with David and Lynn, but he's stayed with us before too."

"Right. Buck was with us last night when we were playing poker."

"Correct. And Buck stayed with us last night. But later this morning, Eric got all paranoid about Buck for some reason. He went to the closet—you know, the closet right next to the garage door."

"Yeah. I know the closet."

"Well, that's where we keep the shotgun and—"

"Lori, don't tell me Eric shot and killed Buck. No way, man."

"No, he didn't. Buck's fine. He's back with David and Lynn, and that's where the shotgun is too."

"OK. Whew."

"But he would have killed Buck. He got the shotgun out and went after Buck. Luckily, I had removed all the shells in the gun last week on account of how Eric was acting."

"Man, good move, Lori." Then I remember telling her, "Always trust your instincts."

"Thanks. Well, I thought I'd let you know."

"Absolutely. Call me any time."

"Eric's calmed down since. He feels bad about what happened."

"Lori, you have to be honest with me, now. Do you feel safe?"

"I'm OK. It's his new meds. The combination's off. We're going to see another doctor tomorrow."

I encouraged Lori to get out of there if she didn't feel safe. And when I got home, I started researching everything I could about TBIs.

Lori called me toward the end of that early September week. "Eric's new meds seem to be helping. David and Lynn came by to visit too, and they brought Buck. Eric cried when he saw his beloved Buck, and he kept telling him, 'I'm sorry. I'm so sorry, Buck,' all while Buck was wagging his tail, happy to see Eric."

I remember things calming down for the next couple of weeks, but then in late September, Lori called me with some more bad news.

"Dean. It's Lori."

"Hi Lori. What's up? Give some good news about Eric," I remember saying. I was in my home office doing research for a media agreement.

"I'm afraid I have bad news."

"Oh no."

"You won't believe this."

"Oh? What happened?"

"About thirty minutes ago, I heard the weirdest sound from our garage. I open the door to the garage and what do I see? Eric, standing in his wheelchair. He was wearing his prosthetic legs, which he rarely wears. He had a chainsaw in his hands and he was hovering over the Chevy Equinox. He was actually cutting, or attempting to cut, the top off of the Equinox. I yelled at him, 'Eric! What are you doing, for crying out loud!' I had to yell because that chainsaw was buzzing away. He turned around, looked at me smiling, and said, 'Oh, hi honey. Hey, I just thought we should have a sunroof on the Chevy. Pretty neat, huh?' I argued with him, and finally he came to his senses. I dunno, Dean. This is getting crazy."

I remember telling her, "Wow. That's nuts."

"Yes it is. I think his meds are helping, but that too is problematic. And he's always forgetful."

"Oh boy," I said.

"Dean, I gotta tell you, it's constant watching over him, reminding him of basic stuff. I dunno if I can handle all of this."

I didn't know what to tell her, then she said, "I told Eric I need a break. I'll be with him on weekdays, but I need Friday night off and the weekends off."

I said nothing.

"Eric's parents are such sweethearts. They agreed to look over him Friday nights, and they'll rotate during the weekends, so at least there'll be someone here to watch him. Saturdays and Sundays are their real busy days for real estate, showing properties and hosting open houses, but it will work out."

"That's understandable," I told her.

"Now I gotta get some estimates on our Equinox. I doubt insurance will cover such a crazy, deliberate act."

I kept researching all I could about TBIs, and I kept texting Eric just about every other day. Our phone conversations had become borderline incoherent, so I had resorted to texts. Lori also kept me abreast of things, informing me that the weekend arrangement with Eric's parents was working. And both of Eric's parents were also calling me and texting me with updates at least once a week.

Then came some sad news in early October. It was the deer-rut season, and there were quite a few deer around Eric's new house. One morning, good old protective Buck had one such deer in his sights, and he started chasing the animal. His chase led him to cross a road—or attempt to cross a road—and that's when a big Dodge Ram pickup, with not enough time to react, struck the great German shepherd.

"Buck didn't die right away," is how Mr. Holzer explained it to me in a phone call, "but there was no way Buck would make it. We had to put him to sleep. Helluva thing, Dean. Buck chasing a buck deer. That's how he died."

"I'm sorry to hear that, Mr. Holzer. How's Eric handling this?"

"Oh he's devastated, Dean. Eric loved Buck."

"I know it."

"Hey, well listen. We're gonna have Buck cremated, then his ashes will be buried here behind Eric's house this weekend. I'm sure Eric would love to see you."

I agreed to visit that weekend. Besides, I wanted to discuss my research with the Holzers, research that I thought could help Eric.

I drove up to Bangor—my usual leave work around two on Friday afternoon, arrive in Bangor around midnight, stay at the Courtyard by Marriott, drive back to Maryland on Sunday. Barbara wanted to come, but she's a real stickler about Covid-19 and crowds.

I met Eric, his parents, and Wendy at Eric's house that Saturday. Lori was there too. We all engaged in small talk—I remember Wendy telling me she was enjoying

Cornell—and then it was time for Buck's funeral. Eric, in his wheelchair, held the urn with the ashes, and all of us, wearing protective masks, made it down from the deck to some twenty yards from the river. A short, white Christian cross, not yet erected, was to the side of a headstone that read *In Loving Memory of Our Beloved Buck. Man's Best Friend. March 8, 2008–October 6, 2020.* Next to the headstone was a small grave with an equally small hill of dirt.

Ms. Holzer said a short prayer, and upon its completion, Mr. Holzer instructed Eric to place the urn in the grave.

"Sure, Dad, but I wanna scatter some of Buck's ashes in the river where he'll float forever."

"Sure thing, son. Go ahead."

Lori guided Eric and his wheelchair to the river's edge. Once she stopped pushing the wheelchair, Eric lifted the urn above his head in such a way that the steady breeze caught the top layer of ashes and blew them toward the river, so still it almost seemed without current. Lori then spun and guided Eric and the wheelchair back to the gravesite, where Eric bent down with the urn and said, "Lori, I can't reach down to place the urn." Lori took the urn from Eric and gently placed it in the grave, and then each family member grabbed a handful of the cold dirt and released the dirt onto the urn.

Ms. Holzer quietly recited another prayer as her husband, armed with a shovel, filled the grave with the loose earth. It was Ms. Holzer who gave the white cross to Eric for him to hold straight as Mr. Holzer, using the back end of the shovel, pounded the cross in place.

We all returned inside Eric's house, where Ms. Holzer served us cookies and coffee. Eric and I chatted a bit— his speech not always coherent—and when Eric excused himself to go to the bathroom, I figured it was the best time to pitch my researched plan. All of us, including Wendy and Lori, were around the table.

"Mr. and Ms. Holzer, have you guys—"

"Please, Dean. You know the deal by now. Call us David and Lynn."

"Sure. Well, David and Lynn. I've being doing a lot of research on traumatic brain injuries and I think Eric should give marijuana a try."

I remember there was silence, then Wendy chimed in with, "I've read about that. The army is spending money on medical research for PTSD and TBIs. Marijuana seems to help."

"Correct," I said. "And the FDA not too long ago approved a cannabis-based drug to help mitigate the symptoms of epilepsy. You know, Lynn and David, it's not easy getting a drug approved by the FDA. Plus here in Maine, this state has legalized marijuana not only for medicinal purposes but also for recreational use. I've got a printout of establishments legally selling marijuana. It's a business now, with business licenses, the payment of taxes, everything's properly regulated. And I'm keeping my eye on whether medical marijuana will be available at VA medical centers. It's not right now, but maybe things will change."

Mr. Holzer sipped his coffee then said, "Well gosh darn it, I'm a fan of giving something a try. Eric's up and down, always prescribed different combinations and doses. I say we give pot a try."

And so it was. Lori informed me that in less than a week after my proposed solution, Mr. Holzer purchased some marijuana for Eric from a small licensed shop, and Eric then showed noticeable improvement, especially with conversation ability, but also with demeanor and mood. I also noticed the improvement in my phone conversations with Eric—much, much better; much more coherent and pleasant.

Then, out of the blue in late October, came a concern— not a major problem, but a concern nonetheless, one that once again I thought I might be of assistance with. I received notice of this concern in a phone conversation with Eric.

"Dean, buddy. How's my basic training battle buddy hanging?"

"Fine, Eric. How are you? What's up?"

"Good. Things are good. But I have to tell you, Bud, I'm bored. My energy levels are good, and 'bout a week ago I started writing poetry, man."

"That's great, Eric."

"Yeah, it's cool knowing that I can now write, thanks to pot. But here's the thing: I can't write poetry all day."

"Yeah, that's understandable."

"I'm too sedentary, Dean. Sitting and reading and writing. I'm not getting enough exercise. Besides, as you know, Lori's only here four days a week. The sex has dropped down big time."

I thought for a while, then something came to me. "Eric, you remember our conversation with Colonel Gadson, about finding purpose in living?"

"Yeah. I think so."

"So what you're telling me is your problem is you're not getting enough exercise?"

"Correct. And not enough sex. Which is related to exercise."

"OK, so the solution to your problem is to get more exercise."

"Right. And also more sex."

"Well, Dean, I can't help you in the sex department—that's between you and Lori, but as far as exercise, just get more exercise."

"Dude, exercise is hard when you don't have legs."

"OK, here's what I recommend. I've seen this before on TV. Sports is the answer, man. Play sports. It won't be football, though. But basketball. Also ice hockey. You can pick up these sports, Dean. And if they don't have them in Bangor, maybe you could start the sport leagues yourself. I'm telling you, I've seen basketball games where the players are all in wheelchairs. With hockey, they're on some sort of sled."

Two weeks after that conversation, Eric told me he formed such a basketball league in Bangor. "We're two teams of three players each, Dean, and we play twice a week. Not all veterans, but mostly veterans. We don't play full court, just half-court. Right now we don't have a referee, but I think I'll have one by next week. Dave Belanger. He's from our Guard unit."

"That's great Eric. Congrats. Well done."

"Yeah, and guess who the league's top scorer is?"

"Uh, let me guess. Would that be the one and only Eric 'Top Dawg' Holzer?"

"Bingo, buddy. I've developed a nice little hook shot that's killer. Especially when I'm driving to the basket from the right side."

Eric also told me he was looking into ice hockey. "But it's hard to get ice time at Alfond Arena. Hoops, we play either at Bangor High School or UMaine, and they don't charge us anything."

This was all welcomed news, such an improvement with Eric. But then, in what seemed to be a roller-coaster ride of success inevitably followed by failure, came time for yet another downturn. A very personal problem. This one too—at least my initial knowledge of it—came in the form of a phone conversation. I remember it was a Friday night, and Barbara and I were watching a movie on Netflix when Eric called.

"Dean, I'm hurting, man." And I could tell he was because I heard him sniffling, like he had been crying.

"What's up?" I sensed it was hard for him to talk. "Eric, what's up? Tell me."

"Oh Dean, I don't know anymore. Just when things are looking up, another fucking setback surfaces."

He started crying.

"Eric, you can tell me, man. You can tell me anything."

"Oh it's personal," he mustered.

"Like I said, you can tell me anything."

More crying, then, over tears, he eked out, "Dean, can you come visit me this weekend?"

I thought about it, the eleven-hour drive.

"Sure. I'll be there tomorrow."

And I was. I arrived at Eric's house late Saturday afternoon, and we spoke over beers. I could tell he was nervous, and also hesitant, maybe embarrassed about something. He started crying.

"What is it, Eric? I'm here, Bud. I'm here for you, man. You can tell me anything."

More silence, more crying. He pointed to his midsection, but I wasn't getting it. His face was red.

"What is it, Eric?"

He pointed again, and I asked him again, "What, Eric? What is it?"

He gathered himself, then he took a swig of beer. "I ... I ... I lost two legs in combat, man. Now the only leg I've got ain't functioning. My junk don't work." He took another gulp of beer. "Erectile fucking dysfunction. E fucking D." He started crying.

Christ, I felt for him. What's a man without his manhood? But like the previous obstacles Eric had to deal with, this one too had a solution. The concentration-incoherence problem seemed to be solved with marijuana. The lack-of-exercise problem was solved by a basketball league. Now Eric's sole leg ain't working, and I figured technology was the answer. "I got this, Eric. Problem, problem solved."

"It's so fucking embarrassing, Dean. And don't tell anyone. Not my parents. Not Wendy. Not Barbara. Even Lori doesn't fucking know. She's become distant, man. We haven't done it in … in a long while. And now I can't do it anymore."

I took a sip from my beer. "I got you covered, Eric." I started googling Viagra and VA centers and Bangor, Maine. In minutes, I discovered the Department of Veterans Affairs covers ED.

"You're covered, dude. Problem solved. You'll be back in the game soon. Little purple pills called Viagra. You'll be up and back in the game in no time, stud muffin."

We laughed.

"Shit, I'm already one hundred percent disabled."

"Yeah, well, you won't be disabled no longer in the you-know-what department." We laughed some more. "You've got great VA facilities here in Bangor. Two, in fact. Just drive up, get your prescription, then pick up your Viagra at a local pharmacy. Everything comes in bags—nobody has to know your medications. VA picks up the tab. Problem solved."

And it was. In subsequent phone conversations with Eric, he informed me, "Everything's working," "everything's up," "rock solid."

November was around the corner, and Eric's focus became unmistakable—politics, specifically the reelection of President Donald J. Trump. I had my views, he had his. The only thing was, on the subject of politics, there was never any gray area with Eric. He was a Trumpster all the way, while I wasn't. I couldn't vote for Trump, nor did I.

Eric, he was convinced President Trump would be reelected, so right up to the November 3 election, he was gung ho and confident. But when Vice President Biden won, Eric was all in with those who disputed the results. He spent hours scouring the internet, researching analysis of the results and why, in his view, voter fraud carried Biden to victory. Politics often slipped into our phone conversations, with Eric always maintaining the election was stolen from Trump. He also was adamant that Trump was right about pulling our troops from Afghanistan. On that subject, I reminded Eric that it was President Trump who some time earlier "left it to the generals" to figure out the American position in Afghanistan, and that now some of the military brass had reservations about a full pullout.

"Trump knows what he's doing," I remember Eric telling me passionately over the phone. "I didn't lose my legs for a lost cause, buddy. We've been in the 'Stan basically two decades. We built roads to improve commerce, built schools to educate children, to include girls getting an education. We've trained and equipped the Afghan Army. We've set them up for success, and now it's time to pull out."

"I agree, Eric," I told him. "I'm just saying some of the higher-ups have reservations about a full pullout."

"Trump's ahead of everybody. The Afghan Army can handle the Taliban. Maybe the Taliban will share a bit of power with the Afghan government, but they won't be in control. Nobody wants the Taliban in charge, and besides, the Taliban doesn't enjoy popular support."

Shortly after that phone conversation came news of Cecilia and the Trump rally. And then a stray bullet ended Eric's life.

―――――――――――――――

After a comfort break that included a gas-up in Massachusetts, Cecilia and I arrive in Bangor a few hours before midnight. I park at the Courtyard by Marriott, retrieve my luggage, which includes my suit for Sunday's funeral, and Cecilia and I enter the hotel.

"How about we meet at the lobby entrance for continental breakfast tomorrow morning, Cecilia? Say, nine thirty?"

"OK," she says. "Sounds like a plan."

We get our separate rooms, and I keep thinking about Eric as I fall asleep.

Saturday, as agreed, Cecilia and I meet for breakfast. We're both dressed in jeans, sweaters, and heavy topcoats since today's high is expected to hit only the low thirties. We're both wearing protective masks as well, on account of Covid-19. I notice the blue-ink letters tattooed on each of Cecilia's left-hand fingers, T-R-U-M-P, and tattooed on her left forearm, also in blue ink, is Make America Great Again.

Over cereal and toast and coffee, we discuss today's game plan of visiting the Holzers for lunch and giving them the urn with their son's ashes.

We're at the Holzers' beautiful home at 11:30 a.m. I notice more cars than usual in the semicircular, snow-covered asphalt driveway. I park at the end behind a black Cadillac Escalade with a New Hampshire license plate, and Cecilia and I exit my car.

The Holzer house, which I've been in a couple times, is a recently remodeled, three-thousand-square-foot Victorian painted light gray with white trim. An attached three-car garage with pitched roof is to the left, and the humongous yard of nearly three acres is blanketed with a solid coat of white snow about six inches in depth.

We're greeted at the door and invited in by Mr. Holzer, and I immediately notice Wendy and Ms. Holzer, both with tears in their eyes, sitting at the kitchen table surrounded by folks I've never met. Everyone, like us, is wearing a mask.

Mr. Holzer immediately introduces me to his brothers and sisters, their families, and his wife's siblings and nephews and nieces. I notice there's no sign of Lori.

"Oh, and let me introduce you to the most recent family addition," Mr. Holzer tells me. "Buck Two, also known as Buck Junior," he says loudly. He whistles, and out from the kitchen area comes a dark German shepherd, young in appearance, considerably smaller than his deceased namesake. The dog, wagging his tail, stands next to his master.

"Buck Junior, say hello to Dean," Mr. Holzer says, petting the dog. "And Dean, this here is Buck, not full grown but getting there, just like our blessed deceased Buck was once a young'n."

I pet Junior, then Wendy offers Cecilia and me cups of coffee, which we both accept. After introductions— this is the first time the Holzers are meeting Cecilia—I walk next to Mr. Holzer and ask if I can have a moment with him in private. He agrees, and we meet next to the front door entrance, out of earshot from the crowd in the kitchen.

"I have the urn, sir. In my bag." I had received the urn from Cecilia after breakfast.

"Thank you, Dean," Mr. Holzer says matter-of-factly. "And please, call me David or Dave."

I manage to say "OK," then he says, "I'll take it."

I place my coffee cup on a nearby table near the foyer, unzip my bag, and hand him the urn. Mr. Holzer simply says "thank you" and heads upstairs with it. He's back down the stairs in a couple of minutes.

"Thank you, Dean, for all you've done for Eric. Do you and Cecilia want to join us for lunch? We've got plenty of food. Grilled cheese sandwiches, tomato soup, pizza, wings, and cookies. Comfort food on a cold day."

"I'm actually OK, sir. Uh, I mean, David. Lemme ask Cecilia."

I walk over to Cecilia, who was next to Ms. Holzer and Wendy.

"Please join us for some finger food," Ms. Holzer says. "We've made a lot of food, and the pizza is from Papa Gambino's."

I look over at Cecilia, who says, "Actually, I'm not all that hungry."

"Well, at least have some more coffee and cookies, dear."

And so we did. Like Cecilia, I wasn't all that hungry. The food—all laid out on platters in the large kitchen— looked great, but I actually wanted to save some room for my two favorite eateries, McLaughlin Seafood and The Fiddlehead Restaurant.

After the coffee and cookies, Cecilia and I politely leave the Holzer home, but before we do, we confirm with Wendy. "The funeral's tomorrow at Bangor High School Auditorium, two p.m., correct?"

"Yes, correct. And be sure to arrive somewhat early, as we're expecting a large crowd."

While walking back to my Subaru, I ask Cecilia, "Well, what do you have planned for the day? Do you want me to drive you back to the hotel?"

"Sure, that sounds good. Drop me off at the hotel."

"Are you going to stay there all day?"

"No. I already checked and they've got Uber here. I'll explore Bangor later this afternoon. What about you?"

"I plan on visiting my two favorite restaurants. Just eat and chill. Read the news on my iPhone while enjoying a craft beer. You've got my number, right?"

"Yeah."

"Cool."

I drive Cecilia back to the Courtyard by Marriott, and confirm with her that I'll be in the lobby at one o'clock tomorrow, giving us plenty of time to drive and park at the high school auditorium for Eric's funeral.

'm at the McLaughlin Seafood restaurant enjoying a lobster roll and a glass of the house red (no craft beer here). It's one-thirty in the afternoon, and I send some texts of my culinary delight to Barbara. My thoughts then shift to Eric, especially that fateful day this past Wednesday. With that, I decide to google President Trump's lengthy remarks, and in seconds I find his speech, verbatim. I start reading while enjoying my late lunch.

Well, thank you very much. This is incredible. Media will not show the magnitude of this crowd … We have hundreds of thousands of people here and I just want them to be recognized by the fake news media … The media is the biggest problem we have as far as I'm concerned …

You don't concede when there's theft involved …

Because if Mike Pence does the right thing, we win the election … They've used the pandemic as a way of defrauding the people in a proper election … And you're the real people, you're the people that built this nation …

Because right over there, right there, we see the event going to take place. And I'm going to be watching. Because history is going to be made …

I had to beat Stacey Abrams. And I had to beat Oprah, used to be a friend of mine. You know, I was on her last show, her last week, she picked the five outstanding people … Believe it or not, she used to like me …

I brought a lot of our soldiers home …
They're in countries that nobody even
knows the name, nobody knows where
they are. They're dying. They're great, but
they're dying. They're losing their arms,
their legs, their face. I brought them back
home, largely back home. Afghanistan,
Iraq.

Boy, I remember right then and there that a few of
the protestors went straight to Eric and lifted him in his
wheelchair above their heads, and the biggest guy who
was part of the lifting crew yelled, "Here's one of those
great heroes. Back home. God bless him." Eric was all
smiles.

Remember, I used to say in the old days:
"Don't go in Iraq. But if you go in,
keep the oil." We didn't keep the oil. So
stupid. So stupid these people. And Iraq
has billions and billions of dollars now in
the bank. And what did we do? We got
nothing …

As this enormous crowd shows, we have
truth and justice on our side. We have a
deep and enduring love for America in our
hearts. We love our country … Together,
we are determined to defend and preserve
government of the people, by the people
and for the people. Our brightest days are

before us. Our greatest achievements, still away … And we fight. We fight like hell. And if you don't fight like hell, you're not going to have a country anymore … the best is yet to come.

So we're going to, we're going to walk down Pennsylvania Avenue. I love Pennsylvania Avenue. And we're going to the Capitol, and we're going to try and give. The Democrats are hopeless—they never vote for anything. Not even one vote. But we're going to try and give our Republicans, the weak ones because the strong ones don't need any of our help. We're going to try and give them the kind of pride and boldness that they need to take back our country.

So let's walk down Pennsylvania Avenue. I want to thank you all. God bless you and God bless America. Thank you all for being here. This is incredible. Thank you very much. Thank you.

I take a sip of wine. I think back at the fateful day. The president's long speech, the enthusiastic crowd. I remember saying right after Trump's rambling, as the crowd started moving forward, "Gang, I'm heading out. I'm not interested in this, and I don't have a good feeling about it." And Eric saying, "Ah, don't be a pussy, Dean."

I finish my wine, and I pay for the lobster roll that no longer exists on my plate but rather occupies my fully satisfied tummy. Next, my plan is to head over to The Fiddlehead Restaurant for some more reading and a late dinner of beef tenderloin topped off with a pint of Cadillac Mountain Stout. And I'll be thinking of Eric.

On the day of the funeral, I park at Bangor High School Auditorium, and Cecilia and I exit my Subaru. The time is one-thirty in the afternoon, and the place is filled with cars, pickup trucks, minivans, and SUVs. I see plenty of folks filing in the auditorium, and everyone, including Cecilia and me, is wearing a protective facial mask. I'm dressed in my navy-blue suit, white shirt, blue tie, and my winter overcoat. Cecilia is wearing beige dress pants, a light orange shirt with matching sweater, and a white winter coat. We get in the steadily moving line, and we're in the auditorium in five minutes.

Inside the warm building, I notice a rectangular table in the middle of the gym floor with two sports jerseys draped at each end of the table. In the center of the table, between the jerseys, is Eric's urn, gold in color. I notice to the right of the table is a dark-brown wooden podium, and to the right of it are Wendy and her parents seated in metal chairs. To the left of the table is a military Honor Guard comprised of three soldiers, the middle one holding the American flag guidon. I decide to walk up to the Holzers and pay them my respects. Cecilia follows me.

"My condolences, Wendy," I tell her, speaking through my mask. Like everyone in the auditorium, she too is wearing a mask.

"Thanks," she tells me, loud and clear. "I'd shake your hand, but it's probably not a good idea on account of Covid."

"Understandable," I tell her, and Wendy then says, "Dean and Cecilia, after this ceremony, family and friends are invited to the burial site where we'll scatter Eric's ashes behind his house. You both are invited to come."

"Thank you," I say. "We'll be there," and I next give my condolences to Eric's parents. Cecilia does the same.

I find seating spaces on a nearby front-row bleacher. Everyone keeps about six feet from one another.

A tall, bald man wearing his army dress blues walks up to the podium. I recognize him—it's Colonel Roy, Eric's National Guard commander.

"The ceremony will commence in five minutes," he says, and he stays at the podium. To my left, about twenty yards away, I notice an African American man in a wheelchair. He's dressed in a gray business suit. I immediately recognize him as Colonel Gadson.

Minutes pass as a few more well-wishers file into the auditorium. Some walk up to the Holzers to exchange greetings but most do not. I estimate the crowd at maybe four hundred.

"Good afternoon, guests, friends, family," says Colonel Roy. "Today, we send our goodbyes and respects to a great American, Eric Holzer, scholar, athlete, soldier, friend. Eric excelled at everything he did. We'll miss him terribly, but he will always be in our thoughts and prayers. What great memories we have of him."

There's polite applause, then Colonel Roy says, "Attention to orders," and Eric's National Guard unit members, to my left, some hundred feet away, all stand up at the position of attention. The center Honor Guard soldier, upon Colonel Roy's order of "Ready, colors, present arms," now raises the flag guidon up, straight and erect, the two soldiers to his sides raising their M16s parallel to their erect bodies. Everyone in the auditorium is now standing.

"The Secretary of the Army has reposed special trust and confidence in the patriotism, valor, fidelity, and professional excellence of Eric D. Holzer. In view of these qualities, he is posthumously promoted to the rank of sergeant."

Colonel Roy shows a framed certificate of promotion to the crowd, and the military members yell "Hooah." That's followed by applause, then a soldier from the unit, also in dress blues, walks up to Colonel Roy, takes the framed certificate, and takes the few steps to Ms. Holzer and hands her the certificate.

Colonel Roy looks at the crowd. "Attention to orders. To all who shall see these presents, greetings: This is to certify that the President of the United States of America, pursuant to authority vested in him by Congress, has awarded the Purple Heart, established by General George Washington at Newburgh, New York, August 7, 1782, to

Sergeant Eric D. Holzer for military merit and for wounds received in action on May 20, 2021, in Afghanistan."

That citation too is in a framed glass case, and the same soldier walks up to his commander, gently grasps the case, and presents it to Mr. Holzer.

We're all still standing when Colonel Roy once again says, "Attention to orders" and proceeds to read the citation for Eric's Bronze Star: "Eric D. Holzer, United States Army, distinguished himself by exceptionally meritorious wartime service as a journalist, Public Affairs Detachment, Multinational Corps, Afghanistan, Bagram Air Base, Afghanistan, from March 27, 2020, to May 21, 2020, during Operation Freedom's Sentinel." That award certificate is also framed in a glass case and presented to Eric's sister, Wendy. "To the colors," orders Colonel Roy, and the soldier holding the flag guidon lowers the American flag.

"Please be seated," says Colonel Roy. "Now I'd like to introduce another great American. Bangor, put your hands together for retired Colonel Gregory Gadson." Loud applause follows. Colonel Gadson wheels his wheelchair to the front of the podium, and Colonel Roy hands him the portable microphone.

"Thank you. Thank you. Thank you all. Wow, what a great crowd. I am sure I speak for so many of you here today who were incredibly saddened first by Eric's combat injuries, and next by his sudden death this past week at our nation's Capitol. I had the pleasure of meeting Eric when he was recuperating at Walter Reed, a facility I'm familiar with because of my similar injuries. I can tell you that Eric was a true hero, because whatever he excelled at, it wasn't about him—it was always about a higher purpose. In sports, it was Eric doing everything he could to help his team win. He achieved his dream of becoming a professional athlete, signing a contract with the Houston Texans but postponing that hard-earned dream of his so he could serve his nation in combat, a cause he also believed in. Like Pat Tillman, Eric was a true champion, and I was honored to know him. May he rest in peace."

There's loud applause and a standing ovation for Colonel Gadson as he hands the mike to Colonel Roy and wheels himself back to the bleachers.

"Thank you, Colonel Gadson," Colonel Roy says. "Words spoken like a true champion. Now next I'd like two individuals to come up here. Bangor, give it up for your own Frank Scagliotta and UMaine Coach Joe Harasymiak."

The two fit men, dressed in business casual attire with open collar white shirts, walk up to the podium as the loud applause continues.

"Thank you. Thank you. As you know, Eric wore the same number, number 23, here at Bangor High and at UMaine. Joe and I are here to tell you that because of Eric's greatness on the football field, we honor him by retiring his number."

There's loud applause.

"Like the great Chicago Bull, the one and only Michael Jordan, no one will wear number 23." He hands the microphone to the other coach, who I assume was Eric's college coach.

"Same at UMaine, folks. We're retiring Eric's number 23. Eric was a special player, right up there with the great Lorenzo Bouier. It's only fitting that we retire his number."

Again, a standing ovation and loud applause mixed in with the chant "Holzer, Holzer," as the two coaches grab the respective jerseys from the table and present them to Eric's family. Some fifteen feet from Wendy, I see an older gentleman taking photos, and I learn, from nearby patrons, that the old man is Buzz Labbe of the *Bangor Daily News*.

"OK, next, we'll hear from another all-star," Colonel Roy says. "Wendy, I know you have a few things to say. Wendy Holzer, ladies and gentlemen."

The crowd applauds as Wendy, wearing black pants and a white blouse, steps behind the podium, the microphone already in its stand.

"Thank you. Eric was special to us all, and I was proud to be his sister. Some of you may know that in the last six months, Eric developed an interest in poetry. I'll read one of his favorite poems shortly, but before I do, our family thanks you all for your prayers and generosity and support. A special thanks to our local National Guard unit—thank you, Colonel Roy; thank you, Color Guard; thank you, all soldiers, for coming. Our family wishes to thank the Wounded Warrior Project, Habitat for Humanity, our local Lowe's and Home Depot, and D'Angelo Builders who designed and helped build Eric's house. And right after this celebration, in this here gymnasium, Papa Gambino's will be catering a midafternoon luncheon for all of you. Free pizza and sodas for everyone on behalf of my great parents, David and Lynn of David and Lynn Realty."

The crowd starts chanting, "David and Lynn, David and Lynn," and Wendy looks over at her proud parents.

"And now, one of Eric's favorite poems. We dedicate it to Eric, and also to our beloved dog, Buck, who, many of you know, died a couple of months ago. It is only fitting that later today, Eric's ashes will be spread next to our beloved Buck's. This poem is titled 'Man's Best Friend.' Eric didn't write this poem, but he read it often, and it was his favorite.

> My friend is loyal and eager to please.
> I'd sit in my chair, his head on my knees.
> I'd stroke his back and pat him on the side.
> The things he would do filled my heart with pride.
> …
> Unconditional love is what he gave me.
> I went the last mile.
> I was there to the end.
> I know now why they called him "Man's Best Friend."

"Thank you," Wendy says, and she walks to her seat as the crowd applauds and chants, "Wendy! Wendy!"

"We'll now hear from Eric's father," Colonel Roy says into the microphone. "Bangor, give it up for the real estate man, David Holzer. David Holzer, ladies and gentlemen."

There's loud applause, and Mr. Holzer, dressed in a black suit, white shirt, and red tie, walks to the podium.

"Thank you," he says, smiling. "Thank you."

There's silence—a long pause. I look at Mr. Holzer, and I sense something's wrong. He looks down. I notice his shoulders shaking a bit, and his face turning red. His left hand now covers his eyes.

I think he's crying.

Yes, Mr. Holzer is crying, and the place is dead quiet. He wipes his tears with his left hand and finally musters, "He was a great son … We … we loved him."

The shoulder shrugs again, and he cries some more. He looks at me. I'm taken off guard, but I keep looking at him. He hand-signals me to come forward, and I start walking to the podium.

"Can you say a few things about Eric?" he asks when I reach him.

"Absolutely," I say.

Mr. Holzer heads back to his seat as Wendy stands and pats him on the back. The crowd starts clapping and gives Mr. Holzer a standing ovation, chanting, "David, David." Colonel Roy looks at me, smiling. I know he doesn't know who I am, but I smile back and give him a thumbs up. Surprisingly, I'm calm, and I plan my remarks to include a few I know by heart. Like the other speakers, I lower my face mask and approach the podium and microphone.

"I'm Dean Leonard, and Eric was my best friend. I can tell you that Eric was the most talented person I've ever met. We did basic training together, and he was by far the best soldier, which is why he won all the awards. We then did AIT together, and I can tell you Eric was one of the best writers in the program, certainly the best writer when it came to feature writing and sports writing."

I pause for a second or two.

"Ernest Hemingway once said, 'Every man's life ends the same way. It is only the details of how he lived and how he died that distinguish one man from another.'"

I quickly pause again.

"The details of how Eric lived his life were rich indeed. The star football player who made it into the NFL. The dedicated patriot who insisted on serving his country in combat. A man of action who got things done. Like Wendy, I end with a poem, this one by the great Walt Whitman:

> O Captain! My Captain! our fearful trip
> is done,
> The ship has weather'd every rock, the
> prize we sought is won,
> The port is near, the bells I hear, the
> people all exulting.
> While follow eyes the steady keel, the
> vessel grim and daring;
> But O heart! heart! heart!
> O the bleeding drops of red,
> Where on the deck my Captain lies,
> Fallen cold and dead.

"Thanks for the many memories, Eric, and rest in peace. You may have died, but your spirit lives forever. Thank you."

I walk back to my seat as the crowd applauds, and I quickly glance at Mr. Holzer, who gives me a thumbs up.

"This concludes our ceremony," Colonel Roy says. "For invited friends and family, Eric's ashes will be scattered next to Buck's shortly. And for everyone else, please enjoy the free pizzas and refreshments."

I walk toward Wendy and her parents, and Cecilia walks behind me.

"Thank you for those kind words," Ms. Holzer tells me as I stand next to her. Her mask is still on. "Yeah, thanks for bailing me out, Dean," Mr. Holzer says.

"Glad I could help."

"And you're attending the spreading of the ashes, correct?" Mr. Holzer asks me.

"Absolutely."

"But first, have some of that great Papa Gambino's pizza."

"OK," I say.

As I make way to the pizza tables that are quickly being set up by wait staff and soldiers, I notice Cecilia placing her iPhone next to the microphone, and suddenly Frank Sinatra singing "My Way" is playing:

> And now the end is here.
> And so I face the final curtain.
> …
> I did what I had to do.

I saw it though without exemption.
I planned each chartered course.
Each careful step along the by way.
And more, much much more.
I did it my way.

Cecilia and I get in line for pizza and sodas. I think her song selection was spot on.

━━━━━━━━━━━━━━━━━━━━━━━━━━━━━━━━

Cecilia and I are in my Subaru heading to Eric's house. "That was a nice ceremony," I tell her.

"Yes. Yes it was. And great pizza."

"Absolutely," I say. "And nice touch with the Sinatra song."

"Thanks."

"I plan on leaving for home right after the spreading of the ashes."

"Sure, no problem. Drive safely," she says. "I've decided to stay here for a while, maybe a week or so. I like Bangor. And I don't mind winter."

"We checked out of the hotel this morning. Do you need a ride back to it or some other hotel?"

"Nope. No worries. I'll be fine. Uber works well. And I'll get another hotel room. I think I might visit Portland later this week."

"How will you get there?"

"Bus. Or maybe a friend. I've got a friend in Boston. She might visit me this week."

We park behind some thirty vehicles at Eric's house, and we exit my car. It's cold, and there's a lot of snow in the yard, but the roads and driveway are well ploughed. Cecilia and I start walking, following a small crowd to the back of the house. Up ahead, unmistakably, I see Lori, Eric's girlfriend, or rather ex-girlfriend. I didn't see her in the high school auditorium—maybe she was there, maybe she wasn't. I'm thinking she was because she had to be invited here, right? This is awkward, me and Cecilia here, walking behind Lori. We're walking at the same clip, so we're not gaining any ground on her; we're not catching up.

We arrive at the back of Eric's house. We're part of a crowd of maybe fifty folks encircling Buck's gravesite next to the Penobscot River, which has thin ice on its edges. I see the Holzers—David, Lynn, Wendy—standing next to a priest who's holding a Bible, and to their left is Colonel Roy in front of a seven-member firing party, National Guard members with their M16s pointed toward the river. To the far end of the firing party is a bugler, his brass bugle to his side. Everyone is wearing a facial mask, including Colonel Roy and the priest, and everyone is wearing an overcoat, save Colonel Roy and the funeral detail. It's getting dark quick as the sun fades toward the west over a hilly tree line.

I notice that David is holding Eric's urn with the top off, and Lynn and Wendy each have a hand on the urn. The priest opens his Bible to a bookmarked page, and the Holzers begin to scatter and spread the ashes on a thick coat of snow next to Buck's grave and the Christian cross. The priest reads loudly:

> By the sweat of your face
> you shall eat bread,
> till you return to the ground,
> for out of it you were taken;
> for you are dust,
> and to dust you shall return.

Colonel Roy, standing next to the firing party, orders "Ready," and the soldiers chamber the blank rounds into their M16s. On Colonel Roy's order of "Aim," they aim their M16s at a forty-five-degree angle toward the river, all in unison. On "Fire," the soldiers fire the first volley, and Buck Junior, considerably bigger than when I last saw him, barks twice at the sound of gunfire but goes quiet for the next two rapid volleys of "Ready, aim, fire, ready, aim, fire."

With the last volley, the bugler plays taps, and it is then that the tall Colonel Roy, holding a triangular glassed-encased American flag, walks up to Ms. Holzer and says, "On behalf of a grateful nation. This flag flew in Kabul, Afghanistan." He hands her the triangular case.

The crowd starts to form a line heading toward the Holzers to shake their hands. I notice Lori up ahead, shaking hands with David, and when she turns to Lynn, they embrace. I notice Lori and Wendy also hug.

"Dean, on second thought, I could use a ride back to the Marriott," Cecilia tells me as we move forward with the line. "I'll stay there for a while."

"Sure," I tell her. "No problem."

Cecilia and I say our goodbyes to the Holzers. As I pass Wendy she tells me, "We'll have a headstone for Eric this spring, once the snow melts."

"That's great," I tell her.

"We'll bury his urn there too."

"Let me know when that's scheduled, Wendy. I'd like to be here for it."

"Absolutely. We'll call you. Probably in April."

Cecilia and I head back to my Subaru. It's hard to grasp that not too long ago, I was here, in the back of Eric's house, for Buck's funeral. Eric, in his wheelchair, struggling with the dog's urn, Lori helping him to lower the urn to bury it. Now Eric's dead, and some of his ashes are partly in the river and partly in the snow that will melt and turn to water and enter the earth next to Buck's grave.

We enter my car, and I turn the ignition to warm up the engine. A thought hits me. "Cecilia. Can you open the glove compartment? There's a photo in it."

"Sure," she says. She opens it and quickly holds up the photo.

"Check it out. It's one of my best memories of Eric."

"Nice," Cecilia says, smiling. She turns the photo and reads the back. "Soccer diplomacy. Living the Dream. Eric Holzer. Afghanistan, May 4, 2020."

"I got it from Wendy, actually," I tell her.

"Cool," she says.

"It's Eric handing a soccer ball to a young Afghan boy. The handwritten note in the back is his handwriting. I've got a digital copy too. Want a copy?"

"Sure."

I turn on the heater and reach for my iPhone. I quickly find the photo and text it to Cecilia. I then text Barbara who's back in Annapolis: "Funeral went well. I'll be home tomorrow, Monday. I'm taking that day off. I plan on staying in Scranton, Pennsylvania, tonight. Miss ya. Love ya. Dean."

I pull onto the road and head in the direction of the Marriott. I'm thinking of Eric, of us back in basic and AIT, his pride when he signed the NFL contract, his happiness and purpose when he was serving in Afghanistan. His accident. His wheelchair. His therapy. His house and Chevy Equinox. His lows and depression. His upswing, thanks to pot and sports and Viagra. I think of the plans we had made over beers and poker, plans for this new year, 2021, hopefully free of Covid-19, plans of climbing Mount Katahdin, Maine's highest point. Plans of maybe ice fishing in northern Maine. Plans of seeing the Red Sox and Patriots play. As I'm driving, my thoughts shift to Eric's favorite writer, Philip Roth, and that famous tragic character of his in *American Pastoral*, one Seymour Levov. The world is your oyster! True, but boy can life change on you. Eric is like Seymour. Everything's perfect for the all-American, but then BAM! Your life changes. But Eric bounced back, he sure did. He found purpose with sports, and President Trump and his reelection efforts. And he found Cecilia. He died happy. My best friend died happy.

I notice Cecilia looking at her iPhone, searching for a music video. She's not wearing her earbuds, which is cool, and I recognize the song immediately. Another of Cecilia's apropos selections, this time "Ashes to Ashes" by David Bowie:

> I'm happy, hope you're happy too
> I've loved all I've needed to love
> Sordid details following."
> …
> Ashes to ashes, funk to funky
> We know Major Tom's a junkie
> Strung out in heaven's high
> Hitting an all-time low …

Printed in the United States
by Baker & Taylor Publisher Services